La chiave nel latte

Translated from Italian

Elvezia's House
Alexandre Hmine

Translated from Italian by
Elena Pala

First published in English by Strangers Press, Norwich, 2022
part of UEA Publishing Project

Originally published in Italian © Gabriele Capelli Editore, 2018

The unpublished manuscript of this text in Italian, *La chiave nel latte*, won the Studer/Ganz Prize, in 2017

All rights reserved
Author © Alexandre Hmine, 2018
Translator © Elena Pala, 2022

Printed by
Swallowtail, Norwich

Editorial assistance
Lily Alden, Erin Maniatopoulou and Emma Seager

Proofread by
Senica Maltese

Cover design and typesetting
Glen Robinson (aka GRRR.UK)

Design Copyright © Glen Robinson, 2022

The rights of Alexandre Hmine to be identified as the author and Elena Pala to be identified as the translator of this work have been asserted in accordance with the Copyright, Designs and Patents Act, 1988. This booklet is sold subject to the condition that it shall not, by way of trade or otherwise, be lent, resold, hired out, stored in a retrieval system, or otherwise circulated without the publisher's prior consent in any form of binding or cover other than that in which it is published and without a similar condition including this condition being imposed on the subsequent purchaser.

ISBN: 978-1-913861-45-2

EA
PUBLISHING
PROJECT
press

Alexandre Hmine

Elvezia's House

Translated by

Elena Pala

MOHAMMED V AIRPORT, CASABLANCA, 1976 (1395 HIJIRI')

A Moroccan girl takes her seat on an intercontinental flight. She is seventeen and pregnant, running away to avoid bringing dishonour on her family.

Her married sister will meet her in Switzerland, where she has already been living for a few years.

Vezio, Canton of Ticino, 1976

Seven months after giving birth, the teenage mother leaves her baby son in the care of an elderly widow.

ELVEZIA'S HOUSE

I see Elvezia. Her grey, slicked back hair, her twinkling narrow eyes, the bulging veins on her neck. She is wearing a dark knee-length skirt, woollen socks and clogs. She is sitting at the head of the table, slouching. I see my aunt and her husband too, standing in front of the sideboard in the living room. She's dressed in black, gold sparkles on her brown skin. He's wearing a light-coloured shirt and is almost bald. They're all looking at the floor, smiling amiably. They're looking at me.

I am on the rug, maybe sitting, maybe lying down.

Maybe it's just a photo, maybe my mother took it.

※

I see the bars on my cot bed, the chipped wall paint, the stuffy, dimly lit room. The floor creaks under Elvezia's clogs. She's wearing a white nightgown with a flower print. She comes closer, grabs the bunched-up duvet at my feet and pulls it over my shoulders. I say nothing, curl up on one side, slot my arms between my knees and wait. She strokes the back of my neck. She likes that, feeling my curls in her hand. Me, I like running my fingers on the back of her hands, tracing the web of her veins, gently pressing down from time to time.

Shapes and colours are fading away. I can hear Elvezia.

'Thy will be done. On earth as it is in Heaven...'

Her words come to me muffled, perhaps because I've hidden my head under the duvet, or perhaps I'm falling asleep. I have learnt both the Our Father and Hail Mary. I repeat in my head, 'as we forgive those who trespass against us...'

I hear these prayers every day. Elvezia sometimes asks me to recite them with her, often before meals on a Sunday. Sometimes she recites them by herself, under her breath, her head bowed.

'And lead us not into temptation...'

I hear the floor creaking, Elvezia's bed springs groaning.

She pulls the cord. All dark.

Amen.

※

I'm playing in the courtyard. I can see the patched-up tarmac on the road, my trike abandoned in a corner. The bright blue shutters are left slightly ajar so the light — softened — can still reach the living room. I can see the metal letterbox on the wall, the wood grain and frosted glass of the entrance door, the tilt window in the bathroom. The grey façade of another house towers over one side of our courtyard. I see the low wall and the spikes on the railing, the woodshed stacked with logs, the steps leading down to Elvezia's allotment.

Across the wire fence sits a building (How many storeys? I can't count) where another set of neighbours live. There's a tree in the middle of their garden. Neglected, the grass grows tall. On our side of the fence, the little allotment where Elvezia grows vegetables, and more steps.

I'm chasing our cat, maybe.

Maybe I trip.

I tumble.

I'm in tears at the bottom of the steps.

I've scratched my hands. I'm bleeding and my head is pounding. I call Elvezia, crying for help.

Now I'm sitting on her lap. I mustn't sniffle or I'll swallow my own snot. 'Bofagh sü,' says Elvezia, encouraging me to blow on the bruise while she massages it with a herbal balm.

※

I remove the draft excluder, open the French window and sink my boots into the fresh snow.

I breathe in the crisp mountain air and admire the landscape: the silhouette of the peaks blurring into the milky sky above and sweeping meadows below. I walk across the balcony towards the balustrade, pat the soft blanket of snow on it, then wipe out a chunk with my forearm. The road that leads down to the square is also carpeted in snow – a long, pristine white strip. The farmer's son is digging a path through his courtyard.

I like how the snow perches on the electricity cables.

I move to the nearest corner of the balcony, but I can't see Ur Stradón, the main street, because the snowplough threw up a barrier as it cleared the road — I can just about make out the wire fence. Further up the street, I can see rocky outcrops, the wooden fence of the playground, a tree.

I cross to the other side and observe the neighbours' garden: it's completely covered in a white blanket of snow that softens the bumps on the ground, hiding shrubs and things.

I read the time on the bell tower clock: the cafe's not open yet.

I press the fresh snow into a ball and aim at Elvezia. I miss, but I've startled her and she turns to look at me, panting and massaging her back. She tells me off. 'Wrap up warm' she says, 'l'è un frecc dala madona' — it's bloody cold out here. Then she carries on shovelling.

☀

I can see the carefully folded napkins, the orange Ovaltine tub, the ceramic sugar bowl and the two plates where Elvezia has laid out Zwieback rusks with butter and jam — cherry, blackberry, plum, or strawberry. I have to wait for her without swinging my chair back and forth, sat up straight with my hands resting on the table. I tuck my napkin into the collar of my pyjama top.

I can hear her clogs shuffling on the tiles — here she comes, carrying two steaming jugs. She places mine next to my plate, stirs in the Ovaltine and encourages me to blow on it because it's very hot. It's not like I have a train to catch or something.

I blow, compliant.

While we wait for the milk to cool down, she tells me about her late husband — it was he who built the house we live in now — about the long trek to school when she was a child, about her teachers and the packed classrooms.

'Oh, I really am going cuckoo!' she scolds herself when memory fails her.

I like listening to her.

I start whistling. Elvezia frowns, her face darkens. 'Mócala! Stop it! No singing and no whistling at the table!'

That makes me giggle.

'Enough already! Or you'll get a good smack!' she warns, glaring at me.

※

Today Santa Claus is coming in his big boots. He arrives on a tractor.

Sat on the benches, we sing the Christmas song as we wait our turn.

'And if our mammas say we've been good kids, you'll bring us a big bag full of gifts!'

He calls us one by one and hands out bags full of peanuts, tangerines, marzipan and chocolates.

No apples, which means all the children were nice.

My imagination is running wild trying to figure out who is behind the white beard.

Someone says they know.

'Who?'

'It's a secret,' he says, zipping up his lips with his fingers.

※

I'm crouching on the living room rug, lining up colourful magnetic letters in the hope of forming a word. A present, not sure who from. Sat on the armchair next to the stove, Elvezia is reading her newspaper, *La Libera Stampa*. She licks the tip of her fingers before turning each page. Every now and again, she lowers the paper and bends her neck to peer at me over her glasses.

The afternoon light flows in from the two windows.

I rummage in the pile of letters, pick one up, examine it to decide if I'm going to keep it and where I'm going to put it, then call out to Elvezia to read what I've written. She advised me to start with short words — four, maximum five, letters — and to use vowels, but I often build long strings of consonants. I don't listen to her because I enjoy her reaction when the result is unpronounceable.

ASDFGHJKL

She chortles, shakes her head and says, 'No, not like that, you silly boy!'

So I reshuffle the letters and start over: consonant, vowel, consonant, vowel.

MAMA

Elvezia reads and corrects my mistakes.

The wood-fired stove crackles. I see the cast iron and the glass pane glowing orange, the metal tube that climbs up and then ducks into the wall. I'm lying on a blanket, my legs stretched out on the armrest. The cat is resting in the other armchair. It's dark outside.

Next to the treadle sewing machine sits a small radio. It's black, deeper than it is tall. It tells the time too, on four rotating cylinders with white digits.

Usually, Elvezia turns it on when she wants to listen to the news, or on Sunday afternoons for her favourite show, 'La Costa dei Barbari', all about the Italian language.

But it's not Sunday. It must be Saturday. I'm listening to the live commentary of the Swiss ice hockey championship. I support HC Lugano.

I'm dozing. The commentator raises his voice. I'm awake now.

Elvezia tells me to go to bed.

※

He should be here any moment now. I'm waiting for him in the front yard, it's a late spring evening and the sun hasn't yet set. I kick my football against the wall — right foot, left foot. I'm better with my left foot.

I recognise the car. He's back, finally. He lives opposite us. The car slows to a halt and he parks on the main street, right next to our shed. I'm so excited. I kick the ball into a corner and rush to open the gate for him.

I can see him, I see his arms pinning the device against his belly.

He's holding a bag with a box in it.

'Hello, you!' he says when he sees me.

I say hello back and open the front door for him.

'May I come in?' he asks as he crosses the hallway.

She's heard him. Elvezia comes out of the kitchen to welcome him and we all head to my bedroom. He sets it all up for me. After placing the TV on the chest of drawers, he positions the aerial at the top, plugs in the power cord, then switches it on and starts scanning for channels.

'Mind you don't get an electric shock or something!' says Elvezia.

All that's left now is a cloud rising in the sky — grey on blue, smoke without fire — and excitement. Even the red flags with their white crosses fade away, the steps the church the rocks the trees the green blades of grass.

We're celebrating Switzerland's birthday.

Where am I? Sat on the seesaw? On the roundabout? In the sandpit? On the swings? On the steps of the little outdoor theatre? Or maybe I'm running around, restless.

And where are the dogs? I don't see them raging, tearing at the wire fences, can't hear them barking.

The smoke is getting thicker.

This year I contributed too. Elvezia handed me a log.

I'm playing on the ice-cold tiles in the hallway. I've sellotaped two strips of cardboard onto the walls to curve out the corners at one end of the rink; at the other, my slippers bar the way so the puck won't get out. I've built the goals from broken crayons, more cardboard, and orange net bags. I drew the centre line and blue lines with my chalks. The puck was provided by Elvezia: one of those massive black buttons. Each player is made up of three or four Lego bricks, their numbers scribbled on their backs with a black marker. The teams who are not playing are relaxing further down the hallway, under the umbrella rack.

Today HC Lugano is playing Davos. I move the players and provide the live commentary: 'Davos fight with gritted teeth... Icing... Two-minute minor for high sticking... Goooooal!!!'

'Pipe down, you!'

Elvezia reminds me to keep my voice down because it makes her hearing aid screech. She's making caramel pudding — I can smell it; I hear the whisk clattering against the pot.

I lower my voice.

Suddenly, the frosted glass darkens — someone's at the door. I have to pause the match. A friend of Elvezia's comes in. 'Excuse me,' she apologises as she crosses the hallway, trying not to step on the players. I replace the fences and the goal and resume the match with a centre ice face-off.

'Bob Hess zigzags forward, makes short work of the Davos defenders, and it's a goal!!!'

※

There are two grocery shops in town, but we almost always use the one on the main street next to the café. To get in, you need to climb a small flight of stairs and then walk around the side of the building.

Elvezia has sent me to buy bread, a baguette.

I see the faded metal door. When I open it, a bell rings to warn the shop owner, who lives on the first floor. She's old. You have to wait for her to come down, and sometimes she doesn't hear the bell and you have to shout her name or open the door from the inside to ring the bell again.

It's a crammed little room, supplies piled up all over the place. I can't see the bread, she keeps it at the back of the shop. The sweets, however, are displayed on a table to my left and along the counter: Smarties, fruit chews, ChupaChups, chocolate bars – my favourite is milk chocolate.

I'm tempted to steal some while I wait.

※

The phone rings: a powerful sound. I get up to answer. I see the white and orange checked tablecloth, the grey telephone on a coffee table in a corner of my bedroom.

I hear her voice, sweet and caring, asking me how I'm doing, if I need anything, saying 'tomorrow I'll come visit,' asking if I'm happy.

The bathroom is tiny, the door worn and rickety. It creaks and wobbles. You can shut it but there's no lock. Sometimes it swings open when there's a draft, or if someone else is trying to get in. The toilet is right in front of it.

When I'm weeing, I always position my left leg slightly forward and twist my back to the right, as a precaution: I don't want anyone to see my willy.

※

Elvezia is carrying flowers and a watering can. I'm trying to steer my brand-new football — a black and white Tango — on the cobblestones. The ball keeps getting away, especially where the road starts sloping down. We don't meet anyone, only a couple of stray cats. The last stretch of the road is too steep, impossible to control the ball. I pick it up.

The gate is rusty, I have to lean in with my shoulder and push really hard to open it. I walk in, drop the ball, sit on it and wait for Elvezia. She probably stopped by the fountain to fill up the can with fresh water.

I see her coming. She pauses by the entrance and catches her breath, holding on to the gate, then massages her back where it hurts.

Now she's kneeling by her husband's grave. I'm practising dribbling, zigzagging around the tombstones. But there isn't enough room, and the gravel makes it hard to sprint and turn.

I move to the cobbled lane separating the two wings of the graveyard and practise my toe bounce. Heading the ball is hard.

✳

The teacher has gathered us on the green carpet and we are sitting in a circle. I like counting and calculating. I learnt fast. I practise at home, with Elvezia or by myself. I enjoy counting to one hundred as fast as I can, in Italian or in dialect. 'Vün düu trii...'

Our naughty classmate, however, couldn't care less about sums. He picks up the wooden blocks we use in class and throws them at someone – again. The teacher gives him a good smack.

I can see myself there, in the morning light, stacking up wooden blocks and whispering him the answers.

✳

There are always eighteen. I take a slice of black bread from the basket and start breaking it up into morsels to mop up the sauce. Elvezia notices the single ravioli left on my plate. I know she won't force me to eat it, she's resigned by now.

'Are you not finishing that?' she asks.

'No.' I tell her that she got mixed up, that today there were nineteen ravioli. She chortles, then sticks her fork in the remaining ravioli, drops it onto her plate and cuts it in half. The minced meat stuffing oozes out.

✳

It's a balmy, sunny day. Spectators watch the game standing just outside the playing area, or sitting on the bleachers on one side of the pitch.

At schoo,l I'm considered one of the best strikers: I can control the ball, dribble and shoot. But everything's more complicated here – I feel the pressure piling up, my team can't seem to pass me the ball, I run around aimlessly, lost. The defenders all look like invincible evil giants.

I get distracted by people shouting, urging players on, arguing with the referee. Our teacher (who doubles as the coach) wants us to pick up the pace, lose our markers, stop running towards the ball

all at the same time like sheep.

I beat the offside trap, raising my arm. Someone yells to mark 'quellonegro'.

It's like a human wall, roaring and cheering. Some of my teammates join me and jump on my back to celebrate. My knees buckle, I fall. More come, those on the bench too, and flatten me on the grass. My back aches but I'm happy, I'm the hero.

The ref calls us back to the pitch to resume the match — that's enough now. I get up, covered in dirt and white chalk, and make my way towards our end of the field – slowly, to draw out the cheering from the crowd.

'Nicely done, Pelé,' the teacher congratulates me.

※

Here, where it's steeper, I walk in the middle of the road. I move to the right when the dogs start running and barking behind the wire fence, because I'm scared. I know they can't jump over it. But what if they break through?

I hurry past the fence, skip up the steps that lead to the church then turn left. I see red ants crawling on the rocks and a few lizards darting off. I keep walking up a short stretch of tarmacked road, then a dirt road, then a grassy footpath. Aside from the yellow dandelions and white snowdrops, everything around me is green. Grasshoppers chirp frantically.

I can see the bricks now. I follow the path, just a few more steps along the edge of the woods and I'll have reached my destination. Our hut is almost ready — we just need to find one more sheet of corrugated iron to cover the exposed corner.

I lay out my straw mat and sit down.

My friend says Stefano Franscini was a knob and it's because of his stupid law that we all have to go to school now. He lights a fire, I start slicing the cervelat sausages.

※

On Epiphany Day, I'll be in the parish nativity. I've been chosen for a very important role: Balthasar, one of the Three Kings.

I get up to get a closer look. I like my costume. I stroke the fabric and ask Elvezia if she'll be able to finish it today.

She needs to think about it. I look at her imploringly, my hands clasped as if in prayer reaching up to touch her nose. She frowns but nods.

While she sews, I lie back on the rug and play with my magic set. I'm trying to learn the ring trick, but I can't focus. I want to know what the hell 'incense' is.

'It's a plant,' she answers, retrieving the needle from her mouth. 'Now stop distracting me.'

'And what about myrrh?'

Elvezia ignores my question. She frowns. That means I'm annoying her. I give up and keep practising my magic tricks. I wave my magic wand... 'Abracadabra!'

※

I can't see her. Can't see her yet. I hear the car slowing down as it approaches our gate, then the horn.

I hear her drive past our house, hear the automatic transmission as she turns the car around by the post office where the road widens.

The little Christmas tree on its stool towers over the presents piled up around it. Our living room is lit up by colourful flashing lights and by the snow — thick flakes that blot the dark rectangular window. I'm wearing pyjamas, woolly socks and slippers.

I see the advent calendar — the windows are all open and empty, not a single chocolate left. I turn my attention to the presents. I pick them up, shake them and turn them around, trying to guess what's inside. The soft ones are clothes. The medium-sized boxes should be board games, perhaps the ones I asked for: Cluedo, Guess Who, Connect Four. I try to remember which ones are for Elvezia: my mother bought her a silk scarf, my aunt got her perfume. The largest present is mine, anyway. It's so big we had to prop it up against the wall.

It's past midnight. I rip a bit of paper from the furthest corner, but I can only see white cardboard. Excited, I tear a strip of paper across the box.

An ice hockey table! Yes!

I want to look at all the images on the box. I rip it all off. There are scraps of wrapping paper all over the rug.

Standing in the doorway, Elvezia stares at me with uncombed hair and a dark look on her face. I see her nightgown, the blue veins on her calves, her woolly socks and clogs.

She tells me off for wasting the wrapping paper and orders me to pick it all up. 'Then off to bed, and I'd hurry up if I were you!'

※

I'm up early. I stick the numbers on the players' backs and arrange them according to their designated positions. I add the goals, the batteries and the little bulbs that will light up after each goal.

I place the puck in the centre of the rink and challenge Elvezia.

She's carefully folding the wrapping paper that can be reused. Maybe she didn't hear me. I call out again, louder. She says not to shout, she heard me all right. And no, she doesn't know how to play 'the hockay'.

※

I see the grey school bus, the driver manoeuvring to park on the narrow street, the front door, the waiting room, my schoolmates who come back proudly exhibiting their prizes – an apple, a sticker, some toothpaste.

My teeth never win any prizes. I always need a new filling. I can feel the needle prick my gums, I hear the suction tube, the unpleasant noise of the drill. Someone asks: 'How many times a day do you brush?'

When I feel like it, which means almost never. Elvezia reminds me after every meal – 'Teeth!' – but I rarely comply. I go to the bathroom, run the tap and after a few seconds spit out some water.

And that's it.

'Two or three times,' I answer.

They tell me I should wear braces, that I have to discuss it with my parents.

Fat chance.

※

When there aren't any parked cars, we have the whole square to ourselves. It's fun because we can run and kick the ball without risk of denting a car door, and without pausing the game if the ball gets stuck under a vehicle. The only problem is the nearby ravine. Broken beams, rotting shoes, buckets and all manner of toys can be seen littering the slope, and at the bottom even wrecked furniture and mouldy mattresses.

I run as fast as I can but there's nothing I can do — no chance of catching it. The ball disappears. I get to the edge of the ravine, sweating and panting, and I see it getting smaller and smaller as it bounces to the bottom.

I point it out to the others.

They're angry.

'Go after it then!' someone says.

I'm not going down there. I'm scared. There are adders. The railing is rickety. It's too steep. What if I don't make it back up?

※

I stand up and push harder on the pedals to pick up speed before the road starts climbing.

My bike is blue — a racing model with three sets of gears. I have attached a piece of cardboard to the back wheel so it makes a constant rumbling noise, and had a mileometer fitted to the handlebars.

It's scorching hot, one of those summer afternoons when the tarmac melts under the sun and you really should stay home with all the shutters up. But I want to try — I promised — I want to see her.

Cycling past the bridge, I pedal faster and brace myself for the steepest stretch. The mountain and trees provide some shade here. I shift down a gear to climb up the mile long slope that separates me from the nearest town.

I'm panting, my legs ache, and my arms too, a little. Come on, I can't give up now.

I have no intention of getting off my bike and pushing it today.

I get to the top. Now I can relax a little, straighten my back, shift back up to second gear.

The breeze tickles my skin as I ride downhill. I stop pedalling and enjoy the moment. I just have to avoid potholes and cowpats.

Treacherous bends, up and down, I stop a few times to catch my breath and have a sip of water.

Is it my imagination or are those her long blond braids?

But it's all for nothing — because the dog's not barking, the car's not parked outside the house, the shutters are closed.

※

It's become a regular occurrence. I twist the aerial to get a clearer image, call Elvezia and lie back down on my bed.

I can hear her clogs shuffling on the carpet, clattering on the tiles and creaking on the wooden boards.

The shutters are closed. Light from the TV floods my bedroom.

Here she comes. I move the duvet so she can sit more comfortably on the edge of the bed.

I hear her laughter, which often turns into coughing. She enjoys stand-up comedy but dislikes the crass jokes and tiresome catchphrases of some of the participants.

'Oh not this fool again!' she comments, shaking her head. 'What a pillock!... Twit!... Ya big goon!'

As for me, I like the girls in those skimpy costumes. My favourite is called Tinì Cansino.

Eventually I fall asleep.

ELVEZIA'S HOUSE

※

I know that white light! So much white behind the frosted glass! I rush down the hallway and open the door. The thick blanket of snow that fell overnight is almost as tall as me, our front yard practically impassable. I can see the tips of the railing but not the wall. Standing on the doormat, I breathe in the crystal-clear air and wonder how I'll get to the bus stop.

'Come and look!' I call out to Elvezia.

She can't hear me. I find her in the kitchen.

She's been out already, she'll get round to shovelling later.

But...

'There's no rush' she reassures me. The schools will be closed today.

'For real??'

I whoop and cheer like I do when Kenta Johansson scores.

※

I hear the engine. Half an hour late, as usual. She slows down, honks twice and drives on.

When she comes back after turning the car around by the post office, I'm already outside, waiting for her. I see her white Range Rover.

We drive past the town sign. Flanked by trees and rock walls, the road carries on level until the bridge, then climbs up round a hairpin bend by the shooting range.

The grey wall bears the marks of distracted or overly confident drivers – black streaks, chipped bricks.

I look at the abandoned garage. On the wooden door hang a few posters advertising local festivals, bingo nights, football matches.

Sometimes when the road is narrow, we come across the bus going in the other direction. We start fussing. Drops of sweat appear on my mother's forehead, she looks around frantically, jerks back and forth, turns down the volume on the radio and swears in Arabic. I try to help, checking we don't get too close to the railing.

The bus driver waves and thanks us.

I wake up, confused, with one foot on the pillow. I don't like this bed, so big, so hard, so low to the ground. And I don't like the bedroom either, even though it's much bigger than mine. There's no TV, no wardrobe, only a bedside table, a coat rack and a mirror. An exotic landscape on one of the walls — a crystal clear ocean, palm trees and sand. It's their guest room.

I'm hungry. I put on my slippers and head to my mother's bedroom. The door is wide open.

She's asleep on one side, curled up under the bedsheets (which she has entirely to herself), her head resting on her arm. Her boyfriend is lying on his back with his legs splayed out, and he's only wearing his briefs. I can see the dog in the mirrors on their wardrobe doors. He's asleep too.

I walk around the bed, tap on my mother's shoulder to wake her up and whisper that I'm hungry.

'What time is it?' she mumbles, rubbing her eyes. Then I can't quite make out what she says, maybe she's asking me to wait another ten minutes, maybe she goes back to sleep.

※

The vast expanse of the lake is nestled among lush green mountains. The water sparkles in the sun. My hands are shaking on the helm. My mother's boyfriend checks our speed and points out the route. I hear his authoritative, vaguely dissatisfied voice: 'Stay on course.'

I see his brown beard, his wet, slicked-back hair already thinning on the sides, his angular face, the gold chain on his chest.

He adjusts the course. My mother's name is tattooed inside a heart on his bicep.

And where is she? Sunbathing behind us. I can't look back.

※

We already know who's knocking on the door.

'Come in!' we all shout in unison.

The teacher crosses the room to shake his hand. The priest is wearing his usual black frock and glasses — thick lenses, rectangular frames. His hair is thin and grey, with a wayward lock flopping over his forehead. A crucifix hangs from his slim, wrinkly neck. He looks at us and nods, a hint of a smile on his lips.

Elegant and confident, one of my classmates leaves her desk and walks up to the teacher, using her Caran d'Ache box as a tray for her pen and Tippex. The teacher motions me to follow them and says we'll need our pencil cases.

I get up: everyone is looking at me, even the priest. I can see their astonishment. Some of them look jealous.

The teacher leads us into a small, poorly lit room, hands us some worksheets and goes back to the RE class.

'Why are you here too?' asks my classmate.

She seems pleased rather than surprised. I tell her my mother has spoken to the school board to get me an exemption from RE.

'Why?'

'Because I'm a Muslim.'

'What's a Muslim?'

All I know is that Muslims believe in Allah. I tell her that.

※

'Jesus Christ!' grumbles Elvezia, pinching my ear. 'Now you'll get what's coming to you!'

Then, still pinching my ear, she drags me into our front yard. I manage to break free, but not to run away. Barring the way with one arm, she takes off my shoes with the other and inspects them. Livid, she hurls them over the gate, onto the main street.

'That'll learn you!' she snaps, gleefully.

Her hands are covered in shit.

She notices a small brown spot by the doormat. She grabs my ear again — I smell the shit — and pulls me down until my face almost grazes the concrete. I tell her I didn't do it on purpose, I hadn't even noticed.

'God forbid you done it on purpose!' she shouts, pinching harder. Then she lets go and goes back inside.

This is my chance to run, better wait until she's calmed down to settle the matter. I rush to retrieve my shoes before they get flattened by a car.

I can't put them on — damn it — I'm too flustered and my fingers won't undo the laces.

Standing in the middle of the yard brandishing a mop and a bucket, Elvezia pauses to catch her breath. 'Oh, you filthy little slob!' she shouts, realising I'm trying to make a break for it.

She pounces on me wielding the mop over her head. I drop the shoes and leg it, faster, much faster than the Olympian Saïd Aouita.

※

My fingertips on her hips in a clumsy attempt at a hug.

'Gramma, Gramma,' she says in garbled Italian, squeezing — crushing me almost.

I sink into her plump belly. I start giggling, mumble something and wait for her to let go of me.

It's evening. We're at my aunt's, standing in the hallway. To my left, a sideboard covered in trinkets, envelopes and postcards. Although I can't see them clearly, my mother and her sisters are here too — three of them at least, giggling and speaking in Italian, Arabic, French, mixing all the languages up, even within the same sentence.

'Cald! Cald!' says Grandma, shivering in her floaty light blue djellaba. Then she points at the snow covering the pavement and says something in Arabic.

They all laugh. Why?

I can only understand one word: 'Maroc.'

My mother translates: She would like you to go to Morocco with her.

Me? What for?

※

Why am I here? White everywhere: the nurse's coat, my gown,

the sheets, the bedside table, the wall. My brain struggles to kick into gear.

The nurse is holding a pair of small scissors. My mouth and throat are dry. She smiles and starts talking about my willy as she slowly removes the bandages. She asks if it hurts. A tiny bit, yes — I answer — but bearable. She says it's normal on the first day, and that I'll feel better tomorrow.

She chucks the bloodied bandages in the bin and starts cleaning the wound. I smell chamomile. Elvezia sometimes drinks chamomile tea before going to bed.

There it is, in its brand-new look — shrunken, wrinkled, unrecognisable. I see the stitches: black lines, some horizontal some diagonal, zigzagging along the tip, disfiguring it. Will it stay like this?

The nurse spools up the clean bandages and fastens the roll with a pin. 'All good' — she says — 'nice and clean.' Then she leaves.

Was that really necessary?

※

We're walking hand in hand. It's a sunny afternoon, maybe a Wednesday? The town's heaving, we often have to let go of each other to move forward through the crowd. I can't hear what we're saying.

I look around: tall buildings, neon signs, my favourite shop — the Franz Carl Weber toy shop. I look at people looking at us.

Why are everyone's eyes on us?

I look at the men who stare at my mother. They wait for her to make eye contact, study her, size her up almost. When she notices them, she returns their gaze for a few seconds then quickly averts her eyes.

At the café, someone compliments her and tells her we look like brother and sister. She smiles coyly and acts surprised, stroking my curls.

Here's the lake. Here's the shop window, the chairs, the mirrors. We have to climb a few steps. The barber gives us a warm welcome.

He's nice and kind.

We chat a little.

The usual haircut, everyone's favourite. Such lovely curls. Such a nice little black boy. Nice little Moroccan boy. Such lovely curls...

I see them both reflected in the mirror. Him, standing, scissors in hand. Her, sat on an armchair with her legs crossed and her head buried in a gossip magazine.

※

Elvezia gets up and starts rummaging through the various papers piled up on the sideboard. I follow her, looking closely. My mother is waiting patiently at the table. She's wearing skinny jeans and high heels. On the checked tablecloth, I can see her cigarettes and lighter, the ashtray, two coffee pots full to the brim and the sugar bowl. She lifts her chin, twists her neck towards the window and exhales a cloud of smoke.

The ash cylinder keeps getting longer. Dangerously long. I'm worried it'll fall on the rug.

Elvezia hands her my school report. She puts down her cigarette and starts leafing through it.

'Keep going' — we say to her — 'that's the first trimester, move on to the next page.'

I see their beaming faces. They're right next to me, because I can feel kisses and caresses from both sides. Hands pausing on my curls, sliding down to my cheeks.

Well done.

'He's a little genius, this one,' comments Elvezia in her imperfect Italian, relaying my teachers' glowing comments too.

My mother promises to buy me a present: anything I want.

※

We're sitting cross-legged on the steps by the sports ground. Before me, a green slope. Further up, the woods. We're not playing football today, we have to complete our sticker albums.

My classmate argues that 'negri' are useless, pathetic, clumsy. That's why African teams don't get a double page spread.

I'm so annoyed I can't even retort: 'And what about South Korea? What about Canada?'

I refuse to continue swapping stickers with him.

It feels so good when Morocco comes out first in Group F, ahead of all those white players on their double page spreads.

✺

'Juj, tleta,' I repeat, to please her.

The afternoon light floods the living room. On the table, the usual coffee cups, the usual cigarettes, the usual ashtray, the usual sugar bowl. My mother thinks I ought to learn Arabic and she wants to start with numbers.

Is she out of her mind?

'Ar'ba, khamsa, sitta...'

She offered to come up here once a week to teach me.

'How about Wednesday afternoons?'

No.

'Saba'a, tmania, tsa'a...'

I can't see her or Elvezia. I can only hear our voices, numbers, and snippets of conversation. I protest 'I speak the Ticino dialect!', she insists 'This is your language!'.

'Vün, düu, trii... why don't you learn the Ticino dialect instead?'

'Asjnò?' she asks.

Huh?

She smiles. She got mixed up.

'Asjnò?' means 'what?'

I teach her that in our dialect 'asnòn' means 'dunce'. Big dunce, even.

To her, 'dar' means 'house'. To me it's just a preposition — dar Elvezia, at Elvezia's, Elvezia's house.

✺

The party invitations are printed on white folded cards. I take one out from its envelope and open it. The gold writing is slightly embossed. I can see myself in the living room, my feet dangling from the Arab-style sofa — it's red, with gold tassels on the cushions. I turn the invite over in my hands trying to figure out which way is up. I run my finger over the grainy surface, the lines, the incomprehensible letters and words, right to left, left to right.

My finger stops on a familiar bit: 1986.

A small, round metal table. Pale, parched sand littered with cigarette ends. A few beach umbrellas flapping in the wind. A motionless merry-go-round, maybe broken. Palm trees. We meet in a park.

He's neither handsome nor young, with grey hair and spaced-out teeth.

Are we supposed to chat? In which language?

We only have time for a quick coffee, my mother tells him who I am, he's interested, listens, nods.

No one keeps to the lanes, including us. Our taxi driver leans out of the window to complain, jerks forward, honks repeatedly, waves other drivers through. The red light seems no more than a recommendation.

I look at the cars — old wrecks, almost all French makes, at the Moroccans out for a walk, at the beach clubs. Then I look ahead, to where the ocean meets the sky.

She stares into the distance muttering my name: she can't see me but senses my presence. I have a great-grandmother.

'Eji!' she says.

It means 'come here'. I move closer. She can sense it. She puts down her rosary beads on the bedside table and gropes around for my fingers. I sit next to her, offering her my hands. She starts stroking them gently in a slow rotating motion.

I see her glassy eyes, her toothless mouth, the hairs on her chin. She looks older than Elvezia.

How old could she be?

She stops and feels my hands with the tips of her fingers for a few seconds, then starts stroking them again more vigorously, occasionally even with the backs of her hands. And she speaks, even though she knows I can't understand her.

She stops, waiting for me to say something. Waiting...

She starts speaking again, this time so feebly, so haltingly that even the other family members would find her impossible to understand.

I observe her tired body and listen, waiting for someone to come and rescue me.

The palm trees form a funnel. In the middle, a pale sun that looks stuck in there.

The preparations for the evening are in full swing, a frantic to-ing and fro-ing from the bedroom to the bathroom and back again. My mother and aunts rummage through the wardrobe and drawers, helping each other find the perfect outfit.

They want my opinion too.

'Suina?'

She's asking if she looks beautiful. 'Yes, suina, très suina,' I answer.

My aunt lies down on the side of the bed to finish painting her nails ruby red. She's wearing a white bathrobe and her hair is wrapped in a light blue towel, except for a few wet strands that she tried in vain to push back in. She's got big ones like the showgirls you see on TV. But she's not wearing a bra now, so the curve on her chest is less pronounced.

I'm lying on the bed I've been given, playing Nintendo. I have to save people jumping out of a burning building. I move the stretcher.

My aunt gets up, tightens the belt around her bathrobe and fetches her makeup bag from the wardrobe.

'Gagni?' she asks, in a muddle of French and Italian.

I let a few people die, answer 'Oui, bien sûr,' and teach her how to say 'winning' in Italian. Vincere. She giggles and repeats: 'Vinshere, vinshere.'

As she leans over to put the makeup bag on the pillow, I take a peek at her cleavage.

The women are ready: stylish, bejewelled and perfumed. Before they leave, they come over to say goodnight and kiss me quickly on the cheek.

I follow them to the living room. Then I hear their high heels clattering down the stairs and a few incomprehensible words between my mother and the porter.

I climb up onto the sofa, part the curtains slightly and look down. A beige Mercedes is waiting in the middle of the street.

The lights stop flashing and the car drives off.

The TV has only one channel. It's in Arabic.

My grandmother has finished reciting her prayers. She joins me in the living room and sits down on a pouf. She moves her fingers in and out of her mouth to ask if I'm still hungry. 'Lla,' I answer, 'no'. I repeat it again, shaking my head.

'S'chon,' she continues, in a vaguely petulant tone.

What did that mean again?

She wipes the sweat from her forehead. Maybe she's trying to say that it's very hot in Morocco.

'Yes, yes,' I agree, fanning my t-shirt.

She laughs and gesticulates. I can't understand why.

※

The street outside the house is getting busier. Hordes of scruffy children run around after each other, fighting, screaming excitedly. I see young people and little old ladies letting out deafening shrills, completely oblivious to the cars trying to inch through the crowd.

Have they all come for me?

I have no idea who they are.

The horse has arrived too, I rush to tell my mother.

'Yellah!' shouts my uncle from the hallway.

In our dialect, we'd say 'des'ciòlati', hurry up.

We go downstairs hand in hand, but I can't see her. I'm dressed in grey – a custom-made djellaba with matching slippers.

When we emerge from the main door, the deafening shrills

intensify. People taking photos, people clapping.

My mother leads me to the horse. Now I can see her: brown hair falling on her shoulders, blond highlights, blue eyeshadow.

She says something to the rider. He looks at me with eyes wide open, then offers his arm to help me climb into the saddle. The horse paws the ground, twitches, whinnies. I'm uncomfortable and scared. My mother is shouting something at me, but I can't understand.

She gestures me to stay calm.

Slowly, we set off, the crowd clapping along for a few steps.

I'm not scared anymore — now I'm in pain. The horse's mane lashes at my face and there's no way to avoid it. I have to tell my mother. I turn around and motion her to come closer. All that bloody cheering drowns my words.

I shout, gesticulate.

Finally she understands, thank god.

The rider shuffles back on the saddle and draws me closer. That's better — although my cheeks still get lashed every now and again.

There are people everywhere, even watching from the nearby buildings.

The party continues on the balcony, where a gazebo has been set up. I see red and green squares, yellow patterns, tables covered in trays containing sweet and savoury delicacies I've never come across before.

In a corner, the band is playing some Arab tunes.

My aunt explains to me that particular instrument is called an oud.

Well-dressed Moroccans and poorly-dressed Moroccans turn up, some invited, some not.

They chat, eat, and dance.

Now I'm dressed in white — a white fez topped with a crown, white djellaba with gold trimmings and buttons. White and silver cape, white slippers.

They make me sit on a sort of throne that consists of a chair with no legs resting on a sofa, a cushion atop the chair with no legs, and a colourful piece of cloth draped over the cushion.

I'm sat there, gobsmacked, posing for the customary photos and straightening my fez every time it slides down because the crown is too heavy.

Kiss, photo, next please!

Now I'm dancing on a round wooden platform held up by four women who are singing and wiggling their hips.

The guests take turns to deposit large, crumpled notes on the platform.

Swirling in a sea of dirhams, I think of all the toys I'm going to buy.

I'm tired, I want to get down, the music is bothering me, I have to hold the crown in place with one hand to stop it sliding and I'm worried all that wiggling will make the ladies trip over.

More women come to replace them.

The money is for the band.

'Öllapeppa!' Elvezia is amazed.

She has cut through the Sellotape that sealed the box, removed the tissue paper that filled the empty space, unwrapped half a bedsheet, and finally got her hands on her present.

'And what's this supposed to be now?'

I lift the lid and show her, explaining that you can use it to cook meat or fish, 'and you can even put cous cous in it!'

'Cou – what?'

She didn't understand. She turns the present upside down, examining it. I repeat, trying to enunciate: 'cous cous.'

'What's that now?' she frowns, 'speak proper!'

'Cous' (pause) 'Cous!'

She chortles and says nothing, then scuttles into the kitchen to find a spot for the tajine. From there, she yells at me to unpack all my clothes. She's mad because I've ripped the wrapping paper. I retort that it was already ripped in places. She raises her voice:

'The devil's a liar!'

※

Flopping on the duvet after losing his last life, my friend feels something hard sticking into the back of his neck and finds the baby bottle. That seemed like a safe place to hide it – I should have stashed it under the pillow like I always do. My cheeks flush. I drop the controller and pounce on him trying to wrestle the bottle out of his hands. I pin him down, we fight. My voice comes back:

'Give it to me!' I shout, gritting my teeth.

The bed squeaks. I keep wrestling him. From the living room, Elvezia warns that if it's a beating we're after she'll give us a good one.

I give up — I'm not strong enough. I don't stand a chance against his steely grip.

I hear my friend howling with laughter. I see him shake the bottle, the condensed milk bubbles, the red lines on the plastic.

I sit there like a lemon.

※

I get bored here, especially in the mornings. My mother and her boyfriend always sleep in late. I don't even have any friends to play with. I go to the living room and lie on the sofa.

What do I do with myself?

I start rummaging in the drawers. Assorted paperwork, envelopes, photo albums, a copy of the *Divine Comedy* in four volumes, trinkets, tea sets, more trinkets. In the nook underneath the TV, I find some VHS tapes. Some of them with Arabic writing, others with a white label. I pick one at random, put it in the VCR, switch it on and sit back on the sofa.

A close-up of a man's smiling face. Then the camera pans out — he's naked. I look at his body. There's a black fuzzy bush around his penis. A woman kneels before him and starts stroking his stomach, down to his thighs — or is she scratching him?

Back to the man's face again, he shuts his eyes and whispers in a language I don't know — it's not Arabic.

Now the woman's lips are on his penis, she's kissing and licking it.

I walk up to the screen to get a better look, turn up the volume.

'Put something else on!' my mother shouts.

※

Same classroom, same desk layout. I picked the closest chair to the teacher's desk. He's sat there marking our homework. I see his nervous hands — so quick to strike when he gets mad — and his intimidating thick brown beard. He's wearing a light-coloured shirt. I can't see my classmates either side of me.

I'm writing an essay. I wish Italian class would never end, or that we were allowed to continue writing at home. My pen glides tirelessly, I fill pages and pages. I'm describing an unforgettable football match, inspired by my favourite anime *Captain Tsubasa*, but also by the live commentary on Tele Lombardia and other sports shows. I use phrases like 'he gallops across the left midfield', 'excruciating pressure', 'the keeper truly is performing miracles'. I reinvent characters and scenes from the series — sensational stuff like the Tachibana twins' 'deadly catapult kick' or Hyuga's 'tiger shoot'.

I'm having fun. I get to the penalties — I manage to finish the essay on time.

The smiley face the teacher drew sits there on the squared paper at the bottom of the page.

I'm happy.

※

The square is transformed. Under the shade of the old pines, along the low wall where cars are usually parked, the organisers set up the mobile kitchen and bar. I see cases of fizzy drinks, the refrigerator, bread baskets and the huge smoking cauldron. The stone wall is covered in posters. The rest of the square is taken up by wooden tables and benches. Loudspeakers.

'Rosamundaaa, all my love is for you…'

Elvezia gave me a twenty franc note. I dig it out of my pocket, buy a soft drink and grab the cutlery. I'm sitting with the other kids, having fun, waiting for our turn.

'The girl from the mountains is singiiing...'

It's only when they hand me the plate that I'm reminded of what my mother said over the phone: 'They're disgusting animals. Did you know they even eat poo?'

I ask if I can please have the risotto without the Luganighe sausages.

Shock, amazement. They want to know why. Why all the fuss now? I've always eaten them, gobbled them up even. I think of poo. I answer that I'm not very hungry.

'Shut up and eat!' they reply, in unison.

Walking back to my table, I look at the sausages. Sniff them. My mother's words come back to me. It's in our sacred book – the Quran. I don't know what to do.

I wonder if I'll go to hell, what kind of punishment awaits me.

I sit down and eat – sausages and all.

※

He can't believe it. Looking down on us with his blue eyes wide open, he laughs and says I'll show you. He pulls down his shorts and briefs exposing his brown hair down there – he's not embarrassed at all, in fact he's completely unfazed.

He starts masturbating.

His penis has gone hard, some of the veins are bulging.

'That's called a titty fuck,' he says, describing the images on the TV screen.

A what?

The three of us are sat on a dark brown sofa, his feet resting on a coffee table.

The living room is enormous, the furniture very expensive. Behind us, French windows overlook a lush garden.

His movements are faster now, a bit like when we jerk the controller to win a race.

I look at his penis, his red face, the sweat dripping down his neck, the TV.

What is happening? He lets out a squeal and squirts a milky substance all over his legs. A few drops end up on the floor tiles. He seems proud of how far it went.

That's not wee.

Why?

He bursts out laughing — a devilish laugh — and asks if we've been paying attention. We laugh too, unsure what to say.

He rubs the palm of his hand against his thigh once or twice, then jumps up and runs to the bathroom.

He comes back with toilet roll, gets down on his hands and knees and starts wiping.

※

My aunt has come to see me. She's brought me a present, again — she's always very kind and caring. She takes the package out of its plastic bag.

We're standing in front of the sideboard.

'I hope you like them,' I hear her say.

Sadly it's not a videogame — I can tell from the box.

Sitting at the table, my mother and Elvezia look on. I can smell the coffee, see the cigarette smoke. I grab the present and open it, trying not to rip the wrapping paper.

A pair of shoes.

'So?' asks my aunt, eager to know if she's nailed it again. 'They're very trendy,' she adds.

They're hideous. White Ellesse trainers with green polka dots and tassels — they look like ladies' shoes. Everyone would be laughing at me if I wore them — especially in our town.

I don't know if I should say that. Elvezia nods enthusiastically: 'Oh, they're lovely, aren't they?'

※

First, I see a piece of paper covered in stars — some black, some green. I trace a horizontal line, left to right, then down and across to the left, up and across to the right, down and across to the right again, and finally back up to rejoin the first line. Five segments, five points, five triangles. Some of them come out wonky though, different shapes and sizes. The central pentagon is too big.

I get mixed up, take a wrong turn, the lines won't join.

The markers are laid out next to the piece of paper.

Now I see her fingers. I see gold sparkling on her smooth, tanned skin. Bracelets.

I look up. 'Careful' — my mum says — 'Morocco's star only has five points, not six like Israel's.'

She grabs a blue marker and draws a six-pointed star. That's much easier: it's just two overlapping equilateral triangles. I have a go too, with a green marker.

'No, ours is green, the Israeli one is blue. Blue on white.'

I draw a red square with a big white cross in the middle. Switzerland.

The sheet is covered in stars and crosses.

※

The kids sitting on the benches keep an eye on the mountains, the meadows, and the street that leads down to the town square. Those standing with their back against the railings survey the main street. I can usually see them from a corner of my balcony. I spot them and shout down: 'Hiya!'

I join them. Those benches have become a meeting point, especially on summer evenings.

As soon as we hear the noise we stop talking in order to guess who's coming. We recognise most of them by ear by now — unfamiliar bikers are a rare sight. We're particularly fascinated by large motorbikes. The bikers only slow down just in time to tackle the bend — right opposite our bench. They drop down a couple of gears, lean over to one side, then twist the throttle and straighten up again. They fear nothing, not even the bus. Sometimes they wave at us, or nod. If they're not wearing a helmet, we see them smiling or even smoking a cigarette.

We comment — us boys mostly on the motorbikes, the girls on the riders. The rest of the time we gossip.

They want to know why I don't live with my mother.

Someone explained to me that she couldn't look after me because she had to work. I tell them that.

'What about your dad then?'

We're having dinner in a fancy restaurant by the lake. Tonight, I got to choose the place.

I see the little nest of creamy tagliolini. We're talking about football. My mother's friend explains to me how Arrigo Sacchi's 4-4-2 formation works. He says AC Milan is like a tight square that follows a pre-determined set of tactics. They use zonal marking: three of them pounce on an opponent, steal the ball and run off at speed. It's an elaborate show performed by top-notch artists: Baresi, Gullit, Van Basten...

I'm not going to just sit here and listen to this guy talk about Milan as if it was the strongest club on the planet, with the best players and the best manager. What about Zenga's saves — I retort — or Altobelli's goals, or Scifo's pure class.

The guy also talks about the business he runs, about his wife and his two daughters — especially the two daughters. They are both studying to go to university.

After dinner, he slips a fifty or hundred franc note into my hand underneath the table, winking.

His grey hair is beginning to thin.

When we say goodbye, he kisses my mother on the forehead.

A pleasant early-summer evening. A ton of people coming and going everywhere — the street's heaving. I'm leaning against the railings. The sky is still blue.

A Pinzgauer military truck appears. We want biscuits.

'Biscuits! Biscuits!' we shout in French.

The soldiers throw us several packs — we divvy them up between us.

Someone is saying he's going to get himself rejected. Because you have to wake up at the crack of dawn. Because you have to march and obey the bloody Swiss Germans. He'll do what his cousin did: 'if you, like, go proper nuts on them, they'll reject you, send you back home.'

Someone else though can't wait to go and throw hand grenades like Rambo, or shoot a rifle like Tackleberry in Police Academy.

'What about you?'

Me? I shake my head and wag my finger. I'm not Swiss, am I? I've got a Moroccan passport. So no National Service. Which doesn't bother me at all, actually.

'What, not even in Morocco?'

My mother explained to me that citizens who reside abroad don't get called up. Luckily. Because she also said that they pack you off to the desert to fight. Like in a real war.

'Elvezia isn't getting any younger...'

My mother's at it again. I can feel my anger mounting.

It corrupts the stuffy air we breathe, crumbles the plaster on the cracked walls. It's in the whistling noise the old fridge makes, in the bitter-tasting cakes. It's in Elvezia's wrinkled face and her faltering whispers.

It's in our damn tears.

Elvezia is sitting in the armchair now. Her swollen, teary eyes keep wandering upwards. Mine seek shelter elsewhere too — in her emaciated legs, in the fiery orange glass pane of the stove, which kept us warm through so many winters and now huffs and puffs.

She's fallen three times this month.

She can't say them, the words that have invaded and clouded her tired mind for hours, days, months now. She doesn't want to hurt me. We both know it. Neither of us wants to be here. We wish we could put off this moment again, imagine a different reality. Some miraculous alternative that might conquer death, shatter the inevitable.

Instead we sit here, in silence.

※

I hadn't seen her cry before.

She walks up to me — faster now — holding a bowl full of kibble for the cat. She's frowning. I see her bloodshot eyes, deep new wrinkles cutting through her forehead. I didn't expect to find her still awake.

Outside, a hellish wind rattles everything, distracting me. A storm is brewing.

I smile, unperturbed.

When Elvezia lifts her arm over my head, I know she'll give up and won't hit me. Her threats don't frighten me anymore.

I shove her.

The bowl falls on the floor tiles, the kibble rattles out, bouncing and scattering everywhere.

Lying on the carpet, Elvezia mutters something, she complains about the pain in her back, struggling for breath.

A draught comes in from the window frame.

TRANSLATOR'S NOTE

Elvezia's House (original title: *La chiave nel latte*, 'The Key in the Milk') is a fictionalised autobiography of a Moroccan boy who is left in the care of an elderly Swiss widow (Elvezia) by his unmarried teenage mother to avoid scandal back home. Growing up in the 1980s in a little village in the Ticino mountains, the boy must grapple with all the challenges that come with being different from everyone around him. Not that he feels any particular attachment towards Moroccan culture – he doesn't really fit in anywhere.

The novel is a collection of impressionistic memories, snapshots from the narrator's life. In this excerpt, we follow the boy through his early school years, marked by his passion for football and ice hockey, his brushes with racism and prejudice, and the exploration of his sexuality. These, his formative years, are spent with Elvezia, until one day her ailing health makes it impossible for her to continue to look after him. Now a rebellious teenager, the narrator must move in with his biological mother and her new husband.

+SVIZRA is a series of eight chapbooks showcasing contemporary writing translated from the four official languages of Switzerland: German, French, Italian and Romansh. In giving equal visibility to each of the four languages, **+SVIZRA** offers a range of Swiss writing never before seen in English from a diverse group of some of the best authors living and working in Switzerland today, including National Literature Prize winning Anna Ruchat, Iraqi exile Usama Al-Shahmani and treasured Romansh author, Rut Plouda.

+SVIZRA is the result of Strangers Press' latest exciting collaboration with an international group of authors, translators, publishers, designers and editors, all made possible by generous funding from Pro Helvetia.

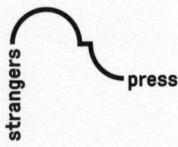

Supported By

University of East Anglia

NORWICH
UNIVERSITY
OF THE ARTS